THE WONDERFUL HISTORY OF
PETER SCHLEMIHL

THE WONDERFUL HISTORY OF

Peter Schlemihl

BY ADALBERT VON CHAMISSO

ILLUSTRATED BY PETER RUDLAND

Story Classics
Emmaus, Pennsylvania

Story Classics is a division of the Rodale Press

Manufactured in England for Story Classics

LIST OF ILLUSTRATIONS

Frontispiece

INTRODUCTION

THE curious history of *Peter Schlemihl*—the man who unthinkingly bartered his shadow for gold and so turned himself into an object of superstitious dread, but refused to sign away his soul even when this would have restored to him, not only his lost shadow, but also the lost joy of living a normal human existence among his fellow men— is one of those 'classic' German tales which hover between the fairy story, irony, whimsy and symbolism, and are characteristic of the German romanticists.

This particular story is among the most famous of its kind. A hundred and fifty years after its first publication it is still peculiarly alive, at least in the German-speaking countries. There, the figure of its unfortunate, clumsy and sensitive hero became part of the same folk-lore from which its creator, Adalbert von Chamisso, had drawn the theme of the uncanny magic properties of a person's shadow. People who have not read the tale again since their school days will often call an unlucky but decent blunderer 'a Schlemihl'. They will think of Schlemihl with a vague feeling of familiarity whenever they come across any of his distant younger relatives in literature, of which there are many, starting with E. T. A. Hoffmann's young man in love who was robbed of his image in the mirror by a spell.

Generations of children have giggled and shuddered at the grotesque episode in the story in which the Fiend cuts off Schlemihl's shadow and neatly rolls it like an umbrella —in Barrie's *Peter Pan*, too, the hero's shadow is cut off, but there is no shudder when Wendy sews it on again. Generations of German critics and historians of literature have produced their interpretations of the symbolic significance behind the fairy tale trappings. The conventional explanation is that the shadow is the symbol of a man's reputation, something which is immaterial but all-important. A more interesting suggestion is that the shadow signifies a spiritual guilt or stain which nevertheless belongs to the complete human personality: 'Decent people are accustomed to take their shadows with them, when they go into the sunshine'. It has been linked with the personal problems of the author, such as his ambiguous position as a leading German poet who was a French aristocrat by birth and who suffered from a sense of rootlessness, of belonging to no country, while the German countries were engaged in the struggle against Napoleon and his France during the 'Wars of Liberation', with their wave of popular nationalist enthusiasm. It was then that *Peter Schlemihl* appeared in print, in 1814.

Indeed, behind the fairy tale devices and the fulsome idiom of the period sounds a realistic note of dry irony and self-mockery. There is in *Peter Schlemihl* a thumbnail sketch of Chamisso himself, presented as a dream which Schlemihl reports to his friend the author: he had dreamt that Chamisso was sitting at his work-table, 'between a skeleton and a bundle of dry plants', in front of three weighty works by eminent naturalists but with a volume of Goethe and de la Motte Fouqué's romantic novel *The Magic Ring* waiting for him on his sofa—and that all the time Chamisso was dead. But the study of nature comes in again, in an opposite sense, when Schlemihl finally achieves consolation for the loss of his shadow, and the loss of human fellowship, by exploring nature as a scientist equipped with Seven League Boots and a searching mind . . . Even a superficial knowledge of Chamisso's background and career will lend a deeper meaning to these odd undertones in a deceptively artless story which was begun as an entertainment for the children of the author's friend.

L. C. A. de Chamisso—who was to call himself Adalbert von Chamisso later on—was born in 1781 at Château Boncourt in the Champagne. After the outbreak of the French Revolution his parents went, like so many other aristocrats, into exile in Prussia, and the young French *émigré* became first a page to Queen Louise at the Berlin Court, then an officer in the Prussian Army. Yet he had been touched by the tremendous upheaval and failed to conform to the pattern of his caste. He joined the circle of Romanticist writers in Berlin, began to publish poems, and studied natural sciences at the University. In 1815, a year after *Peter Schlemihl*, he went with an expedition to Russia and then made a tour round the world, as a serious scientific observer—or as though chasing his lost shadow. Afterwards he became Curator at the Botanical Gardens of Berlin. In the twenties and thirties of the last century he was immensely popular through his cosmopolitan ballads and through his simpler lyrics, of which the song-cycle *Frauenliebe und -leben* ('Woman's Love and Life') is still famous in the settings by Schumann, still a quarry of quotations so familiar to German ears that they seem anonymous proverbs.

Chamisso, however, was not solely a poet of tuneful sentimentality. It was he who translated the challenging poems of the French anti-reactionary Béranger into German, he who first introduced in German lyrics a sober, quiet social realism and new, unheroic subjects such as 'The Old Washerwoman'. It may well be that the training which had taught him to see nature in its diversity of great and small shapes helped him to observe—and to render—the needs of 'little people'. In this, he was a precursor of a new school of poets; he died in 1838, on the eve of the restless decade which led to the revolutionary storms of 1848.

In short, the life and work of this half-forgotten leader of German Romanticism in its last stage was unobtrusively faithful to the gospel of integrity and self-renewal which assuredly lies underneath the whimsical fancies of his Wonderful History of Peter Schlemihl.   ILSA BAREA

CHAPTER I

FTER a fortunate but for me very troublesome voyage, we finally reached the port. The instant that I touched land in the boat, I loaded myself with my few effects, and passing through the swarming people I entered the first, and least, house before which I saw a sign hang. I requested a room; the boots measured me with a look, and conducted me into the garret. I caused fresh water to be brought, and made him exactly describe to me where I should find Mr. Thomas John.

'Before the north gate; the first country-house on the right hand; a large, new house of red and white marble, with many columns.'

'Good.'

It was still early in the day. I opened at once my bundle; took thence my new black cloth coat; clad myself cleanly in my best apparel; put my letter of introduction into my pocket, and set out on the way to the man who was to promote my modest expectations.

When I had ascended the long North Street, and reached the gate, I soon saw the pillars glimmer through the foliage. 'Here it is then,' thought I. I wiped the dust from my feet with my pocket-handkerchief; put my neckcloth in order, and in God's name rang the bell. The door flew open. In the hall I had an examination to undergo; the porter, however, permitted me to be announced, and I had the honour to be called into the park, where Mr. John was walking with a select party. I recognized the man at once by the lustre of his corpulent self-complacency. He received me very well, as a rich man receives a poor devil, even turned towards me, without turning from the rest of the company, and took the offered letter from my hand.

'So, so! from my brother. I have heard nothing from him for a long time. But he is well? There,' continued he, addressing the company without waiting for an answer, and pointing with the letter to a hill, 'there I am going to erect the new building.' He broke the seal without breaking off the conversation, which turned upon riches.

'He that is not master of a million, at least,' he observed, 'is—pardon me the word—a wretch!'

'Oh! how true!' I exclaimed with a rush of overflowing feeling. That pleased him. He smiled at me, and said: 'Stay here, my good friend; in a while I shall perhaps have time to tell you what I think about this.' He pointed to the letter, which he then thrust into his pocket, and turned again to the company. He offered his arm to a young lady; the other gentlemen addressed themselves to other fair ones; each found what suited him; and all proceeded towards the rose-blossomed mount.

I slid into the rear, without troubling anyone, for no one troubled himself any further about me. The company was excessively lively; there was dalliance and playfulness; trifles were sometimes discussed with an important tone, but oftener important matters with levity; and especially pleasantly flew the wit over absent friends and their circumstances. I was too strange there to understand much of all this; too anxious and introverted to take an interest in such riddles.

We had reached the rosary. The lovely Fanny, the belle of the day, as it appeared, would, out of obstinacy, herself break off a blooming bough. She wounded herself on a thorn, and, as if from the dark roses, flowed the purple on her tender hand. This circumstance put the whole party into a flutter. English plaster was sought for. A still, thin, lanky, longish, oldish man, who stood near and whom I had not hitherto remarked, put his hand instantly into the close-lying breast-pocket of his old French grey taffety coat; produced thence a little pocket-book; opened it and presented to the lady, with a profound obeisance, the required article. She took it without noticing the giver, and without thanks; the wound was bound up, and we went forward over the hill, from whose back the company could enjoy the wide prospect over the green labyrinth of the park to the boundless ocean.

The view was in reality vast and splendid. A light point

appeared on the horizon between the dark flood and the blue of the heaven.

'A telescope here!' cried John; and already, before the servants who appeared at the call were in motion, the grey man, modestly bowing, had thrust his hand into his coat-pocket, and drawn thence a beautiful Dollond, and handed it to Mr. John. Bringing it immediately to his eye, he informed the company that it was the ship which went out yesterday, and was detained in view of port by contrary winds. The telescope passed from hand to hand, but not again into that of its owner. I, however, gazed in wonder at the man, and could not conceive how the great machine had come out of the narrow pocket: but this seemed to have struck no one else, and nobody troubled himself any further about the grey man than about myself.

Refreshments were handed round; the choicest fruits of every zone, in the costliest vessels. Mr. John did the honours with an easy grace, and a second time addressed a word to me.

'Help yourself; you have not had the like at sea.'

I bowed, but he saw it not, he was already speaking with someone else.

The company would fain have reclined upon the sward on the slope of the hill, opposite to the outstretched landscape, had they not feared the dampness of the earth.

'It were divine,' observed one of the party, 'had we but a Turkey carpet to spread here.'

The wish was scarcely expressed when the man in the grey coat had his hand in his pocket, and was busied in drawing thence, with a modest and even humble deportment, a rich Turkey carpet interwoven with gold. The servants received it as a matter of course, and opened it on the required spot. The company, without ceremony, took their places upon it; for myself, I looked again in amazement at the man; at the carpet which measured above twenty paces long and ten in breadth; and rubbed my eyes, not knowing what to think of it, especially as nobody saw anything extraordinary in it.

I would fain have had some explanation regarding the man, and have asked who he was, but I knew not to whom to address myself, for I was almost more afraid of the gentlemen's servants than of the served gentlemen. At length I took courage, and stepped up to a young man who appeared to me to be of less consideration than the rest, and who had often stood alone. I begged him softly to tell me who the agreeable man in the grey coat there was.

'He there, who looks like an end of thread that has escaped out of a tailor's needle?'

'Yes, he who stands alone.'

'I don't know him,' he replied, and as it seemed in order to avoid a longer conversation with me he turned away, and spoke of indifferent matters to another.

The sun began now to shine more powerfully, and to inconvenience the ladies. The lovely Fanny addressed carelessly to the grey man, whom as far as I am aware, no one had yet spoken to, the trifling question, 'Whether he had not, perchance, also a tent by him?' He answered her by an obeisance most profound, as if an unmerited honour were done him, and had already his hand in his pocket, out of which I saw come canvas, poles, cordage, ironwork, in short, everything which belongs to the most splendid pleasure-tent. The young gentlemen helped to expand it, and it covered the whole extent of the carpet—and nobody found anything remarkable in it.

I was already become uneasy, nay horrified at heart, but how completely so, as, at the very next wish expressed, I saw him yet pull out of his pocket three roadsters—I tell thee three beautiful great black horses, with saddle and caparison. Bethink thee! for God's sake!—three saddled horses, still out of the same pocket out of which already a pocket-book, a telescope, an embroidered carpet, twenty paces long and ten broad, a pleasure-tent of equal dimensions, and all the requisite poles and irons had come forth! If I did not protest to thee that I saw it myself with my own eyes, thou couldst not possibly believe it.

Embarrassed and obsequious as the man himself appeared to be, little as was the attention which had been bestowed on him, yet to me his grisly aspect, from which I could not turn my eyes, became so fearful, that I could bear it no longer.

I resolved to steal away from the company, which from the insignificant part I played in it seemed to me an easy affair. I proposed to myself to return to the city, to try my luck again on the morrow with Mr. John, and, if I could muster the necessary courage, to question him about the singular grey man. Had I only had the good fortune to escape so well!

I had already actually succeeded in stealing through the rosary, and in descending the hill found myself on a piece of lawn when, fearing to be encountered in crossing the grass out of the path, I cast an inquiring glance round me. What was my terror to behold the man in the grey coat behind me, and making towards me! In the next moment he took off his hat before me, and bowed so low as no one had ever yet done to me. There was no doubt but that he wished to address me, and without being rude I could not prevent it. I also took off my hat; bowed also; and stood there in the sun with bare head as if rooted to the ground. I stared at him full of terror, and was like a bird which a serpent has fascinated. He himself appeared very much embarrassed. He raised not his eyes; again bowed repeatedly; drew nearer, and addressed me with a soft, tremulous voice, almost in a tone of supplication.

'May I hope, sir, that you will pardon my boldness in

venturing in so unusual a manner to approach you, but I would ask a favour. Permit me most condescendingly—'

'But in God's name!' exclaimed I in my trepidation, 'what can I do for a man who—' we both started and, as I believe, reddened.

After a moment's silence, he again resumed: 'During the short time that I had the happiness to find myself near you, I have, sir, many times—allow me to say it to you—really contemplated with inexpressible admiration the beautiful, beautiful, shadow which, as it were, with a certain noble disdain, and without yourself remarking it, you cast from you in the sunshine. The noble shadow at your feet there. Pardon me the bold supposition, but possibly you might not be indisposed to make this shadow over to me.'

He was silent, and a mill-wheel seemed to whirl round in my head. What was I to make of this singular proposition to sell my own shadow? He must be mad, thought I, and with an altered tone which was more assimulated to that of his own humility I answered thus:

'Ha! ha! good friend, have not you then enough of your own shadow? I take this for a business of a very singular sort—'

He hastily interrupted me: 'I have many things in my pocket which, sir, might not appear worthless to you, and for this inestimable shadow I hold the very highest price too small.'

It struck cold through me again as I was reminded of the pocket. I knew not how I could have called him good friend. I resumed the conversation, and sought, if possible, to set all right again by excessive politeness.

'But, sir, pardon your most humble servant; I do not very well understand your meaning. How indeed could my shadow—'

He interrupted me: 'I beg your permission only here on the spot to be allowed to take up this noble shadow and put it in my pocket; how I shall do that, be my care. On the other hand, as a testimony of my grateful acknowledgment to you, I give you the choice of all the treasures which I carry in my pocket—the genuine Spring-root,[1] the Man-drake-root, the Change-penny, the Rob-dollar, the napkin of Roland's Page, a mandrake-man, at your own price. But these probably don't interest you, rather Fortunatus's Wishing-cap newly and stoutly repaired, and a lucky-bag such as he had.'

'The Luck-purse of Fortunatus!' I exclaimed, interrupting him; and great as my anxiety was, with that one word he had taken my whole mind captive. A dizziness seized me, and double ducats seemed to glitter before my eyes.

---

[1] These are references to facts in the popular tales of Germany: as for instance, the Springwurzel, or Spring-root, is found in the story of Rübezahl; and the Galgenmännlein, or Gallows-men, were little figures cut out of a root, said by the dealers in such things in the Middle Ages to be actual Mandrake-roots growing in that shape at the feet of gallows, etc., etc.

'Honoured Sir, will you do me the favour to view, and to make trial of this purse?'

He thrust his hand into his pocket and drew out a tolerably large, well-sewed purse of stout Corduan leather, with two strong strings, and handed it to me. I plunged my hand into it and drew out ten gold pieces, and again ten, and again ten, and again ten. I extended him eagerly my hand.

'Agreed! the business is done; for the purse you have my shadow!'

He closed with me; kneeled instantly down before me, and I beheld him, with an admirable dexterity, gently loosen my shadow from top to toe from the grass, lift it up, roll it together, fold it, and, finally, pocket it. He arose, made me another obeisance, and retreated towards the rosary. I fancied that I heard him there softly laughing to himself; but I held the purse fast by the strings; all round me lay the clear sunshine, and within me was yet no power of reflection.

'For the purse you have my shadow.'

CHAPTER II

AT LENGTH I came to myself and hastened to quit the place where I had nothing more to expect. In the first place I filled my pockets with gold; then I secured the strings of the purse fast round my neck, and concealed the purse itself in my bosom. I passed unobserved out of the park, reached the highway and took the road to the city. As, sunk in thought, I approached the gate, I heard a cry behind me.

'Young gentleman! eh! young gentleman! hear you!'

I looked round, an old woman called after me.

'Do take care, sir, you have lost your shadow!'

'Thank you, good mother!' I threw her a gold piece for her well-meant intelligence, and stepped under the trees.

At the city gate I was compelled to hear again from the sentinel: 'Where has the gentleman left his shadow?'

And immediately again from some women: 'Jesus Maria! the poor fellow has no shadow!'

That began to irritate me and I became especially careful not to walk in the sun. This could not, however, be accomplished everywhere, for instance, over the broad street which I next must approach actually, as mischief would have it, at the very moment that the boys came out of school. A cursed hunchbacked rogue, I see him yet, spied out instantly that I had no shadow. He proclaimed the fact with a loud outcry to the whole assembled literary street youth of the suburb, who began forthwith to criticize me, and to pelt me with mud.

'Decent people are accustomed to take their shadow with them, when they go into the sunshine.'

To defend myself from them I threw whole handfuls of gold amongst them and sprang into a hackney-coach, which some compassionate soul procured for me.

As soon as I found myself alone in the rolling carriage I began to weep bitterly. The presentiment must already have arisen in me, that far as gold on earth transcends in estimation merit and virtue, so much higher than gold itself is the shadow valued; and as I had earlier sacrificed wealth to conscience, I had now thrown away the shadow for mere gold. What in the world could and would become of me!

I was again greatly annoyed as the carriage stopped before my old inn. I was horrified at the bare idea of entering that wretched cock-loft. I ordered my things to be brought down; received my miserable bundle with contempt, threw down some gold pieces, and ordered the coachman to drive to the most fashionable hotel. The house faced the north, and I had not the sun to fear. I dismissed the driver with gold; caused the best front rooms to be assigned to me, and shut myself up in them as quickly as I could.

What thinkest thou I now began? Oh my dear Chamisso, to confess it even to thee makes me blush. I drew the un-lucky purse from my bosom and with a kind of desperation which, like a rushing conflagration, grew in me with self-increasing growth, I extracted gold, and gold, and gold, and ever more gold, and strewed it on the floor, and strode amongst it, and made it ring again, and feeding my poor heart on the splendour and the sound, flung continually more metal to metal, till in my weariness I sank down on the rich heap, and rioting thereon, rolled and revelled amongst it. So passed the day, the evening. I opened not my door; night and day found me lying on my gold, and then sleep overcame me.

I dreamed of thee. I seemed to stand behind the glass door of thy little room, and to see thee sitting then at thy work-table, between a skeleton and a bundle of dried plants. Before thee lay open Haller, Humboldt, and Linnaeus; on thy sopha a volume of Goethe and *The Magic Ring*. I regarded thee long and everything in thy room, and then thee again. Thou didst not move, thou drewest no breath—thou wert dead!

I awoke. It appeared still to be very early. My watch stood. I was sore all over; thirsty and hungry too; I had taken nothing since the evening before. I pushed from me with loathing and indignation the gold on which I had before sated my foolish heart. In my vexation I knew not what I should do with it. It must not lie there. I tried whether the purse would swallow it again—but no! None of my windows opened upon the sea. I found myself compelled laboriously to drag it to a great cupboard which stood in a cabinet, and there to pile it. I left only some handfuls of it lying. When I had finished the work, I threw myself exhausted into an easy chair, and waited for the stirring of the people in the house. As soon as possible I ordered food to be brought, and the landlord to come to me.

I fixed in consultation with this man the future arrangements of my house. He recommended for the services about my person a certain Bendel, whose honest and intelligent physiognomy immediately captivated me. He it was whose attachment has since accompanied me consolingly through the wretchedness of life, and has helped me to support my gloomy lot. I spent the whole day in my room amongst masterless servants, shoemakers, tailors, and tradespeople. I fitted myself out and purchased besides a great many jewels and valuables for the sake of getting rid of some of the vast heap of hoarded up gold; but it seemed to me as if it were impossible to diminish it.

In the meantime I brooded over my situation in the most agonizing despair. I dared not venture a step out of my doors, and at evening I caused forty waxlights to be lit in my room before I issued from the shade. I thought with horror on the terrible scene with the schoolboys, yet

I resolved, much courage as it demanded, once more to make trial of public opinion. The nights were then moonlight. Late in the evening I threw on a wide cloak, pressed my hat over my eyes and stole, trembling like a criminal, out of the house. I stepped first out of the shade in whose protection I had arrived there, in a remote square, into the full moonlight, determined to learn my fate out of the mouths of the passers by.

Spare me, dear friend, the painful repetition of all that I had to endure. The women often testified the deepest compassion with which I inspired them, declarations which no less transpierced me than the mockery of the youth and the proud contempt of the men, especially of those fat, well-fed fellows who themselves cast a broad shadow. A lovely and sweet girl, who, as it seemed, accompanied her parents, while these suspiciously only looked before their feet, turned by chance her flashing eyes upon me. She was obviously terrified; she observed my want of a shadow, let fall her veil over her beautiful countenance, and dropping her head, passed in silence.

I could bear it no longer. Briney streams started from my eyes, and cut to the heart, I staggered back into the shade. I was obliged to support myself against the houses, to steady my steps, and wearily and late reached my dwelling.

I spent a sleepless night. The next morning it was my first care to have the man in the grey coat everywhere sought after. Possibly I might succeed in finding him again, and how joyful! if he repented of the foolish bargain as heartily as I did. I ordered Bendel to come to me, he appeared to possess address and tact; I described to him exactly the man in whose possession lay a treasure without which my life was only a misery. I told him the time, the place in which I had seen him; I described to him all who had been present, and added, moreover, this token; he should particularly inquire after a Dollond's telescope; after a gold interwoven Turkish carpet; after a splendid pleasure-tent; and, finally, after the black chargers, whose story, we knew not how, was connected with that of the mysterious man, who seemed of no consideration amongst them, and whose appearance had destroyed the quiet and happiness of my life.

When I had done speaking I fetched out gold, such a load that I was scarcely able to carry it, and laid upon it precious stones and jewels of a far greater value.

'Bendel,' said I, 'these level many ways and make easy many things which appeared quite impossible; don't be stingy with it, as I am not, but go and rejoice thy master with the intelligence on which his only hope depends.'

He went. He returned late and sorrowful. None of the people of Mr. John; none of his guests, and he had spoken with all, were able, in the remotest degree, to recollect the man in the grey coat. The new telescope was there, and no one knew whence it had come; the carpet, the tent were still there spread and pitched on the selfsame hill; the servants boasted of the affluence of their master, and no one knew whence these same valuables had come to him. He himself took his pleasure in them, and did not trouble himself because he did not know whence he had them. The young gentlemen had the horses, which they had ridden, in their stables, and they praised the liberality of Mr. John who on that day made them a present of them. Thus much was clear from the circumstantial relation of Bendel, whose active zeal and able proceeding, although with such fruitless result, received from me their merited commendation. I gloomily motioned him to leave me alone.

'I have,' began he again, 'given my master an account of the matter which was most important to him. I have yet a message to deliver which a person gave me whom I met at the door as I went out on the business in which I have been so unfortunate. The very words of the man were these: "Tell Mr. Peter Schlemihl he will not see me here again as I am going over sea, and a favourable wind calls me at this moment to the harbour. But in a year and a day I will have the honour to seek him myself and then to propose to him another and probably to him more agreeable transaction. Present my most humble compliments to him and assure him of my thanks." I asked him who he was, but he replied, your honour knew him already.'

'What was the man's appearance?' cried I filled with foreboding, and Bendel sketched me the man in the grey coat, trait by trait, word for word, as he had accurately described in his former relation the man after whom he had inquired.

'Unhappy one!' I exclaimed, wringing my hands, 'that was the very man!' and there fell, as it were, scales from his eyes.

'Yes! it was he, it was positively!' cried he in horror, 'and I, blind and imbecile wretch have not recognized him, have not recognized him, and have betrayed my master!'

He broke out into violent weeping; heaped the bitterest reproaches on himself, and the despair in which he was inspired even me with compassion. I spoke comfort to him, assured him repeatedly that I entertained not the slightest doubt of his fidelity and sent him instantly to the port, if possible to follow the traces of this singular man. But in the morning a great number of ships, which the contrary winds had detained in the harbour, had run out, bound to different climes and different shores, and the grey man had vanished as tracelessly as a dream.

CHAPTER III

OF WHAT avail are wings to him who is fast bound in iron fetters? He is compelled only the more fearfully to despair. I lay like Faffner by his treasure far from every consolation, suffering much in the midst of my gold. But my heart was not in it, on the contrary, I cursed it, because I saw myself through it cut off from all life. Brooding over my gloomy secret alone, I trembled before the meanest of my servants, whom at the same time I was forced to envy, for he had a shadow; he might show himself in the sun. I wore away days and nights in solitary sorrow in my chamber, and anguish gnawed at my heart.

There was another who pined away before my eyes; my faithful Bendel never ceased to torture himself with silent reproaches that he had betrayed the trust reposed in him by his master, and had not recognized him after whom he was dispatched, and with whom he must believe that my sorrowful fate was intimately interwoven. I could not lay the fault to his charge; I recognized in the event the mysterious nature of the Unknown.

That I might leave nothing untried, I one time sent Bendel with a valuable brilliant ring to the most celebrated painter of the city, and begged that he would pay me a visit. He came. I ordered my people to retire, closed the door, seated myself by the man, and, after I had praised his art, I came with a heavy heart to the business, causing him before that to promise the strictest secrecy.

'Mr. Professor,' said I, 'could not you, think you, paint a false shadow for one, who by the most unlucky chance in the world, has become deprived of his own?'

'You mean a personal shadow?'

'That is precisely my meaning.'

'But,' continued he, 'through what awkwardness, through what negligence could he then lose his proper shadow?'

'How it happened,' replied I, 'is now of very little consequence, but thus far I may say,' added I, lying shamelessly to him, 'in Russia, whither he made a journey last winter, in an extraordinary cold his shadow froze so fast to the ground that he could by no means loose it again.'

'The false shadow that I could paint him,' replied the professor, 'would only be such a one as by the slightest agitation he might lose again, especially a person who, as appears by your relation, has so little adhesion to his own native shadow. He who has no shadow, let him keep out of the sunshine, that is the safest and most sensible thing for him.'

He arose and withdrew, casting at me a transpiercing glance which mine could not support. I sunk back in my seat, and covered my face with my hands.

Thus Bendel found me, as he at length entered. He saw the grief of his master, and was desirous silently and reverently to withdraw. I looked up. I lay under the burden of my trouble; I must communicate it.

'Bendel!' cried I, 'Bendel, thou only one who seest my affliction and respectest it, seekest not to pry into it, but appearest silently and kindly to sympathize, come to me, Bendel, and be the nearest to my heart. I have not locked from thee the treasure of my gold, neither will I lock from thee the treasure of my grief. Bendel, forsake me not. Bendel, thou beholdest me rich, liberal, kind. Thou imaginest that the world ought to honour me, and thou seest me fly the world, and hide myself from it. Bendel, the world has passed judgement, and cast me from it, and perhaps thou too wilt turn from me when thou knowest my fearful secret. Bendel, I am rich, liberal, kind, but, O God! I have no shadow!'

'No shadow!' cried the good youth with horror, and the bright tears gushed from his eyes. 'Woe is me, that I was born to serve a shadowless master!'

He was silent, and I held my face buried in my hands.

'Bendel,' added I, at length, tremblingly, 'now hast thou my confidence, and now canst thou betray it—go forth and testify against me.'

He appeared to be in a heavy conflict with himself, at length he flung himself before me, and seized my hand, which he bathed with his tears.

'No!' exclaimed he, 'think the world as it will, I cannot, and will not, on account of a shadow, abandon my kind master; I will act justly, and not with policy. I will continue with you, lend you my shadow, help you when I can, and when I cannot, weep with you.'

I fell on his neck, astonished at such unusual sentiment, for I was convinced that he did it not for gold.

From that time my fate and my mode of life were in some degree changed. It is indescribable how much Bendel continued to conceal my defect. He was everywhere before me and with me; foreseeing everything, hitting on contrivances, and where danger threatened covering me quickly with his shadow, since he was taller and bulkier than I. Thus I ventured myself again amongst men and began to play a part in the world. I was obliged, it is true, to assume many peculiarities and humours, but such become the rich, and, so long as the truth continued to be concealed, I enjoyed all the honour and respect which were paid to my wealth. I looked calmly forward to the promised visit of the mysterious unknown, at the end of the year and the day.

I felt, indeed, that I must not remain longer in a place where I had once been seen without a shadow and where I might easily be betrayed. Perhaps I yet thought too much of the manner in which I had introduced myself to Thomas John, and it was a mortifying recollection. I would therefore here merely make an experiment to present myself with more ease and confidence elsewhere, but that now occurred which held me a long time riveted to my vanity, for there it is in the man that the anchor bites the firmest ground.

Even the lovely Fanny, whom I in this place again encountered, honoured me with some notice without recollecting ever to have seen me before; for I now had wit and sense. As I spoke, people listened, and I could not, for the life of me, comprehend myself how I had arrived at the art of maintaining and engrossing so easily the conversation. The impression which I perceived that I had made on the fair one, made of me just what she desired—a fool, and I thenceforward followed her through shade and twilight wherever I could. I was only so far vain that I wished to make her vain of myself, and found it impossible, even with the very best intentions, to force the intoxication from my head to my heart.

But why relate to thee the whole long ordinary story? Thou thyself hast often related it to me of other honourable people. To the old, well-known play in which I good-naturedly undertook a worn-out part, there came in truth to her and me and everybody unexpectedly a most peculiar and poetic catastrophe.

As, according to my wont, I had assembled on a beautiful evening a party in a garden, I wandered with the lady, arm in arm, at some distance from the other guests, and exerted myself to strike out pretty speeches for her. She cast down modestly her eyes, and returned gently the pressure of my hand, when suddenly the moon broke through the clouds, behind me, and—she saw only her own shadow thrown forward before her! She started and glanced wildly at me, then again on the earth seeking my shadow with her eyes, and what passed within her painted itself so singularly on her countenance that I should have burst into a loud laugh if it had not itself run ice-cold over my back.

I let her fall from my arms in a swoon; shot like an arrow through the terrified guests, reached the door, flung myself into the first chaise which I saw on the stand, and drove back to the city, where this time, to my cost, I had left the circumspect Bendel. He was terrified as he saw me—one word revealed to him all. Post horses were immediately fetched. I took only one of my people with me, an arrant knave, called Rascal, who had contrived to make himself necessary to me by his cleverness; and who could suspect nothing of the present occurrence. That night I left up-wards of a hundred miles behind me. Bendel remained behind to discharge my establishment, to pay money and to bring me what I most required. When he overtook me the next day, I threw myself into his arms, and swore to him never again to run into the like folly, but in future to be more cautious. We continued our journey without pause, over the frontiers and the mountains, and it was not till we began to descend and had placed those lofty bulwarks

'... *she saw only her own shadow thrown forward before her.*'

between us and our former unlucky abode that I allowed myself to be persuaded to rest from the fatigues I had undergone, in a neighbouring and little frequented bathing-place.

CHAPTER IV

I MUST pass in my relation hastily over a time in which, how gladly would I linger, could I but conjure up the living spirit of it with the recollection. But the colour which vivified it, and can alone vivify it again, is extinguished in me; and when I seek in my bosom what then so mightily animated it, the grief and the joy, the innocent illusion—then do I vainly smite a rock in which no living spring now dwells, and the god is departed from me. How changed does this past time now appear to me. I would act in the watering-place an heroic character, ill studied, and myself a novice on the boards, and my gaze was lured from my part by a pair of blue eyes. The parents, deluded by the play, offer everything only to make the business quickly secure; and the poor farce closes in mockery. And that is all, all! That presents itself now to me so absurd and commonplace, and yet is it terrible, that that can thus appear to me which then so richly, so luxuriantly swelled my bosom. Mina! as I then wept at losing thee, so weep I still to have lost thee also in myself. Am I then become so old? Oh melancholy reason! Oh but for one pulsation of that time! one moment of that illusion! But no! alone on the high waste sea of thy bitter flood; and long out of the last cup of champagne the elfin has vanished!

I had sent forward Bendel with some purses of gold to procure for me a dwelling adapted to my needs. He had there scattered about much money, and expressed himself somewhat indefinitely respecting the distinguished stranger whom he served, for I would not be named, and that filled the good people with extraordinary fancies. As soon as my house was ready Bendel returned to conduct me thither. We set out.

About three miles from the place, on a sunny plain, our progress was obstructed by a gay festal throng. The carriage stopped. Music, sound of bells, discharge of canon, were heard; a loud *vivat!* rent the air; before the door of the carriage appeared, clad in white, a troop of damsels of extraordinary beauty, but who were eclipsed by one in particular as the stars of night by the sun. She stepped forth from the midst of her sisters; the tall and delicate figure kneeled blushing before me, and presented to me on a silken cushion a garland woven of laurel, olive branches, and roses, while she uttered some words about majesty, veneration and love, which I did not understand, but whose bewitching silver tone intoxicated my ear and heart. It seemed as if the heavenly apparition had sometime already passed before me. The chorus struck in, and sang the praises of a good king and the happiness of his people.

And this scene, my dear friend, in the face of the sun! She kneeled still only two paces from me, and I without a shadow, could not spring over the gulph, could not also fall on the knee before the angel! Oh! what would I not then have given for a shadow! I was compelled to hide my shame, my anguish, my despair deep in the bottom of my carriage. At length Bendel recollected himself on my behalf. He leaped out of the carriage on the other side. I called him back, and gave him out of my jewel-case which lay at hand a splendid diamond crown, which had been made to adorn the brows of the lovely Fanny! He stepped forward, and spoke in the name of his master, who could not and would not receive such tokens of homage; there must be some mistake; and the good people of the city were thanked for their good will. As he said this, he took up the proffered wreath, and laid the brilliant coronet in its place. He then extended respectfully his hand to the lovely maiden, that she might arise, and dismissed with a sign clergy, magistrates and all the deputations. No one else was allowed to approach. He ordered the throng to divide, and make way for the horses; sprang again into the carriage, and on we went at full gallop, through a festive archway of foliage and flowers towards the city. The discharges of cannon continued. The carriage stopped before my house; I sprang hastily in at the door, dividing the crowd which the desire to see me had collected. The mob hurraed under my window, and I let double ducats rain out of it. In the evening the city was voluntarily illuminated.

And yet I did not at all know what all this could mean, and who I was supposed to be. I sent out Rascal to make inquiry. He brought word to this effect: that the people had received certain intelligence that the good king of Prussia travelled through the country under the name of a Count; that my adjutant had been recognized; and, finally, how great the joy was as they became certain that they really had me in the place. They now saw clearly that I evidently desired to maintain the strictest incognito, and how very wrong it had been to attempt so importunately to lift the veil. But I had resented it so graciously, so kindly— I should certainly pardon their good-heartedness.

The thing appeared so amusing to the rogue that he did his best by reproving words, the more to strengthen the good folk in their belief. He made me a very comical recital of all this; and as he found that it diverted me, he made a joke to me of his own additional wickedness. Shall I confess it? It flattered me, even by such means, to be taken for that honoured head.

I commanded a feast to be prepared for the evening of the next day, beneath the trees which overshadowed the open space before my house; and the whole city to be invited to it. The mysterious power of my purse; the exertions of Bendel and the active invention of Rascal succeeded in triumphing over time itself. It is really astonishing how richly and beautifully everything was arranged in those few hours. The splendour and abundance which exhibited them-selves, and the ingenious lighting up, so admirably contrived that I felt myself quite secure, left me nothing to desire. I could not but praise my servants.

The evening grew dark; the guests appeared; and were presented to me. Nothing more was said about Majesty; I was styled with deep reverence and obeisance Count. What was to be done? I allowed the Count to please, and remained from that hour Count Peter. In the midst of festive multitudes my soul yearned alone after one. She entered late—and she wore the crown. She followed modestly her parents and seemed not to know that she was the loveliest of all. They were presented to me as the Chief Forester, his lady and their daughter. I found many agreeable and obliging things to say to the old people; before the daughter I stood like a rebuked boy and could not bring out one word. I begged her, at length, with a faltering tone, to honour this feast by assuming the office whose insignia she graced. She entreated with blushes and a moving look to be excused; but blushing still more than herself in her presence, I paid her as her first subject my homage, with a most profound respect, and the hint of the Count became to all the guests a command which everyone with emulous joy hastened to obey. Majesty, innocence and grace presided in alliance with beauty over a rapturous feast. Mina's happy parents believed their child only thus exalted in honour of them. I myself was in an indescribable intoxication. I caused all the jewels which yet remained of those which I had formerly purchased, in order to get rid of burthensome gold, all the pearls, all the precious stones to be laid in two covered dishes at the table, and in the name of the queen to be distributed round to her companions and to all the ladies. Gold, in the meantime, was incessantly strewed over the inclosing lists among the exulting people.

Bendel, the next morning, revealed to me in confidence that the suspicion which he had long entertained of Rascal's honesty, was now become certainty. That he had yesterday embezzled whole purses of gold.

'Let us permit,' replied I, 'the poor scoundrel to enjoy the petty plunder. I spend willingly on everybody, why not on him? Yesterday he and all the fresh people you have brought me, served me honestly; they helped me joyfully to celebrate a joyful feast.'

There was no further mention of it. Rascal remained the first of my servants, but Bendel was my friend and my confidant. The latter was accustomed to regard my wealth as inexhaustible, and he pried not after its sources; entering into my humour, he assisted me rather to discover opportunities to exercise it, and to spend my gold. Of that Unknown one, that pale sneak, he knew only this, that I could alone through him be absolved from the curse which weighed on me; and that I feared him, on whom my sole hope reposed. That, for the rest, I was convinced that he could discover me anywhere; I him nowhere; and that therefore awaiting the promised day, I abandoned every vain inquiry.

The magnificence of my feast, and my behaviour at it, held at first the credulous inhabitants of the city firmly to their preconceived opinion. True, it was soon stated in the newspapers that the whole story of the journey of the king of Prussia had been a mere groundless rumour; but a king I now was, and must spite of everything a king remain, and truly one of the most rich and royal who had ever existed; only people did not rightly know what king. The world has never had reason to complain of the scarcity of monarchs, at least in our time. The good people who had never seen any of them, pitched with equal correctness first on one and then on another; Count Peter still remained who he was.

At one time appeared amongst the guests at the Bath, a tradesman, who had made himself bankrupt in order to enrich himself; and who enjoyed universal esteem, and had a broad though somewhat pale shadow. The property which he had scraped together, he resolved to lay out in ostentation, and it even occurred to him to enter into rivalry with me. I had recourse to my purse and soon brought the poor devil to such a pass that in order to save his credit he was obliged to become bankrupt a second time, and hasten over the frontier. Thus I got rid of him.

In this neighbourhood I made many idlers and good-for-nothing fellows.

With all the royal splendour and expenditure by which I made all succumb to me, I still in my own house lived very simply and retired. I had established the strictest circumspection as a rule. No one except Bendel, under any pretence whatever, was allowed to enter the rooms which I inhabited. So long as the sun shone, I kept myself shut up there, and it was said the Count is employed in his cabinet. With this employment numerous couriers stood in connexion, whom I, for every trifle, sent out and received. I received company alone under my trees, or in my hall arranged and lighted according to Bendel's plan. When I went out, on which occasions it was necessary that I should be constantly watched by the Argus eyes of Bendel, it was only to the Forester's garden, for the sake of One alone; for my love was the innermost heart of my life.

Oh my good Chamisso! I will hope that thou hast not yet forgotten what love is! I leave much unmentioned here to thee. Mina was really an amiable, kind, good child. I had taken her whole imagination captive. She could not, in her humility, conceive how she could be worthy that I should alone have fixed my regard on her; and she returned love for love with all the youthful power of an innocent heart. She loved like a woman, offering herself wholly up; self-forgetting; living wholly and solely for him who was her life; regardless if she herself perished—that is to say, she really loved.

But I—oh what terrible hours, terrible and yet worthy that I should wish them back again, have I often wept away on Bendel's bosom, when, after the first unconscious intoxication, I recollected myself; looked sharply into myself—I, without a shadow, with knavish selfishness destroying this angel, this pure soul which I had deceived and stolen. Then did I resolve to reveal myself to her; then did I swear with a most passionate oath to tear myself from her, and to fly; then did I burst out into tears, and concert with Bendel how in the evening I should visit her in the Forester's garden.

At other times I flattered myself with great expectations from the rapidly approaching visit from the grey man, and wept again when I had in vain tried to believe in it. I had calculated the day on which I expected again to see the fearful one; for he had said in a year and a day; and I believed his word.

The parents, good honourable old people who loved their only child extremely, were amazed at the connexion, as it already stood, and they knew not what to do in it. Earlier they could not have believed that Count Peter could think only of their child; but now he really loved her and was beloved again. The mother was probably vain enough to believe in the probability of a union, and to seek for it;

the sound masculine understanding of the father did not give way to such overstretched imaginations. Both were persuaded of the purity of my love; they could do nothing more than pray for their child.

I have laid my hand on a letter from Mina of this date, which I still retain. Yes, this is her own writing. I transcribe it for thee.

'I am a weak silly maiden, and cannot believe that my beloved, because I love him dearly, dearly, will make the poor girl unhappy. Ah! thou art so kind, so inexpressibly kind, but do not misunderstand me. Thou shalt sacrifice nothing for me, desire to sacrifice nothing for me. O God! I should hate myself if thou didst! No—thou hast made me immeasurably happy; hast taught me to love thee. Away! I know my own fate. Count Peter belongs not to me, he belongs to the world. I will be proud when I hear: "That was he, and that was he again, and that has he accomplished; there they have worshipped him, and there they have deified him!" See, when I think of this, then am I angry with thee that with a simple child thou canst forget thy high destiny. Away! or the thought will make me miserable! I—oh! who through thee am so happy, so blessed. Have I not woven too an olive branch and a rose-bud into thy life as into the wreath which I was allowed to present to thee? I have thee in my heart, my beloved, fear not to leave me— I will die oh! so happy, so ineffably happy through thee!'

Thou canst imagine how the words must cut through my heart. I explained to her that I was not what people believed me, that I was only a rich but infinitely miserable man. That a curse rested on me which must be the only secret between us, since I was not yet without hope that it should be loosed. That this was the poison of my days; that I might drag her down with me into the gulph—she who was the sole light, the sole happiness, the sole heart, of my life. Then wept she again, because I was unhappy. Ah, she was so loving, so kind! To spare me but one tear, she, and with what transport, would have sacrificed herself without reserve.

In the meantime she was far from rightly comprehending my words, she conceived in me some prince on whom had fallen a heavy ban, some high and honoured head and her imagination amidst heroic pictures limned forth her lover gloriously.

Once I said to her: 'Mina, the last day in the next month may change my fate and decide it—if not I must die, for I will not make thee unhappy.'

Weeping, she hid her head in my bosom.

'If thy fortune changes, let me know that thou art happy. I have no claim on thee. Art thou wretched, bind me to thy wretchedness, that I may help thee to bear it.'

'Maiden! maiden! take it back, that word, that foolish word which escaped thy lips. And knowest thou this wretchedness? Knowest thou this curse? Knowest who thy love—what he—? Seest thou not that I convulsively shrink together, and have a secret from thee?'

She fell sobbing to my feet, and repeated with oaths her intreaty.

I announced to the Chief Forester, who entered, that it was my intention on the first approaching of the month to solicit the hand of his daughter. I fixed precisely this time because in the interim many things might occur which might influence my fortunes. That I was unchangeable in my love to his daughter.

The good man was quite startled as he heard such words out of the mouth of Count Peter. He fell on my neck, and again became quite ashamed to have thus forgotten himself. Then he began to doubt, to weigh, and to inquire. He spoke of dowry, security, and the fortune for his beloved child. I thanked him for reminding me of these things. I told him that I desired to settle myself in this country where I seemed to be beloved, and to lead a carefree life. I begged him to purchase the finest estate that the country had to offer, in the name of his daughter and to charge the cost to me. A father could, in such matter, best serve a lover. It gave him enough to do, for everywhere a stranger was before him, and he could only purchase for about a million.

My thus employing him was, at the bottom, an innocent scheme to remove him to a distance, and I had employed him similarly before. For I must confess that he was rather

wearisome. The good mother was, on the contrary, somewhat deaf, and not like him jealous of the honour of
entertaining the Count.

The mother joined us. The happy people pressed me to
stay longer with them that evening—I dared not remain
another minute. I saw already the rising moon glimmer on
the horizon—my time was up.

The next evening I went again to the Forester's garden.
I had thrown my cloak over my shoulders and pulled my
hat over my eyes. I advanced to Mina. As she looked up and
beheld me, she gave an involuntary start, and there stood
again clear before my soul the apparition of that terrible
night when I showed myself in the moonlight without a
shadow. It was actually she! But had she also recognized
me again? She was silent and thoughtful; on my bosom lay
a hundred-weight pressure. I arose from my seat. She
threw herself silently weeping on my bosom. I went.

I now found her often in tears. It grew darker and darker
in my soul; the parents meanwhile swam in supreme felicity;
the eventful day passed on sad and sullen as a thunder
cloud. The eve of the day was come. I could scarcely
breathe. I had in precaution filled several chests with gold.
I watched the midnight hour approach. It struck.

I now sat, my eye fixed on the fingers of the clock, count-
ing the minutes, the seconds, like dagger-strokes. At every
noise which arose, I started up—the day broke. The leaden

'. . . *the last minutes of the last hour fell, and nothing appeared.*'

hours crowded upon each other. It was noon, evening—
night: as the clock fingers sped on, hope withered; it struck
eleven and nothing appeared; the last minutes of the last
hour fell, and nothing appeared. It struck the first stroke—
the last stroke of the twelfth hour, and I sank hopeless and
in boundless tears upon my bed. On the morrow I should,
for ever shadowless, solicit the hand of my beloved.
Towards morning an anxious sleep pressed down my
eyelids.

CHAPTER V

IT WAS still early morning when voices, which were raised in my ante-chamber in violent dispute, awoke me. I listened. Bendel forbade entrance; Rascal swore high and hotly that he would receive no commands from his fellow, and insisted in forcing his way into my room. The good Bendel warned him that such words, came they to my ear, would turn him out of his most advantageous service. Rascal threatened to lay hands on him if he any longer obstructed his entrance.

I had half dressed myself. I flung the door wrathfully open, and advanced to Rascal.

'What wantest thou, villain?'

He stepped two strides backwards, and replied quite coolly: 'To request you most humbly, Count, just to allow me to see your shadow—the sun shines at this moment so beautifully in the court.'

I was struck, as with thunder. It was some time before I could recover my speech.

'How can a servant towards his master—'

He interrupted very calmly my speech. 'A servant may be a very honourable man, and not be willing to serve a shadowless master—I demand my discharge.'

It was necessary to try other chords. 'But honest, dear Rascal, who has put the unlucky idea into thy head? How canst thou believe—?'

He proceeded in the same tone: 'People will assert that you have no shadow—and, in short, you show me your shadow, or give me my discharge.'

Bendel, pale and trembling, but more discreet than I, gave me a sign. I sought refuge in the all-silencing gold; and that had lost its power. He threw it at my feet—

'From a shadowless man I accept nothing!'

He turned his back upon me, and went most deliberately out of the room with his hat upon his head and whistling a tune. I stood there with Bendel as one turned to stone, thoughtless, motionless, gazing after him.

Heavily sighing and with death in my heart, I prepared myself to redeem my promise, and like a criminal before his judge, to appear in the Forester's garden. I alighted in the dark arbour, which was named after me and where they would be sure also at this time to await me. The mother met me carefree and joyous. Mina sate there, pale and lovely as the first snow which often in the autumn kisses the last flowers, and then instantly dissolves into bitter water. The Chief Forester went agitatedly to and fro, a written paper in his hand, and appeared to force down many things in himself which painted themselves with rapidly alternating flushes and paleness on his otherwise immoveable countenance. He came up to me as I entered and with frequently choked words, begged to speak with me alone. The path in which he invited me to follow him, conducted towards an open, sunny part of the garden. I sank speechless on a seat, and then followed a long silence, which even the good mother dared not to interrupt.

The Chief Forester raged continually with unequal steps to and fro in the arbour, and suddenly halting before me, glanced on the paper which he held and demanded of me with a searching look: 'May not, Count, a certain Peter Schlemihl be not quite unknown to you?'

I was silent.

'A man of superior character, and of singular attainments—' he paused for an answer.

'And suppose I were the same man?'

'Who,' added he vehemently, 'has by some means lost his shadow!!'

'Oh, my foreboding, my foreboding!' exclaimed Mina. 'Yes, I have long known it, he has no shadow,' and she flung herself into the arms of her mother, who, terrified, clasped her convulsively, and upbraided her that to her own hurt she had kept to herself such a secret. But she, like Arethusa, was changed into a fountain of tears, which at the sound of my voice flowed still more copiously, and at my approach burst forth in torrents.

'And you,' again grimly began the Chief Forester, 'and

you with unparalleled impudence have made no scruple to deceive these and myself, and you give out that you love her whom you have so deeply humbled. See there, how she weeps and writhes! Oh horrible! horrible!'

I had to such a degree lost all reflection that talking like one crazed I began: 'And, after all, a shadow is nothing but a shadow; one can do very well without that, and it is not worth while to make such a riot about it.' But I felt so sharply the baselessness of what I was saying, that I stopped of myself, without his deigning me an answer, and I then added: 'What one has lost at one time, may be found again at another.'

He rushed fiercely towards me. 'Confess to me, sir! Confess to me, how became you deprived of your shadow!'

I was compelled again to lie. 'A rude fellow one day trod so heavily on my shadow that he rent a great hole in it. I have only sent it to be mended, for money can do much, and I was to have received it back yesterday.'

'Good, sir, very good!' replied the Chief Forester. 'You solicit my daughter's hand; others do the same. I have, as her father, to care for her. I give you three days in which you may see after a shadow. If you appear before me within these three days with a good, well-fitting shadow, you shall be welcome to me, but on the fourth day—I tell you plainly —my daughter is the wife of another.'

I would yet attempt to speak a word with Mina, but she clung, sobbing violently, only closer to her mother's breast, who motioned me to be silent and to withdraw. I reeled away, and the world seemed to close itself behind me.

Escaped from Bendel's affectionate oversight I traversed in erring course, woods and fields. The perspiration of my agony dropped from my brow, a hollow groaning convulsed my bosom; madness raged within me.

I know not how long this had continued when, on a sunny heath, I felt myself plucked by the sleeve. I stood still and looked round—it was the man in the grey coat, who seemed to have run himself quite out of breath in pursuit of me. He immediately began:

'I had announced myself for today, but you could not wait the time. There is nothing amiss, however, yet. You consider the matter, receive your shadow again in exchange, which is at your service, and turn immediately back. You shall be welcome in the Forester's garden; the whole has been only a joke. Rascal, who has betrayed you, and who seeks the hand of your bride, I will take charge of—the fellow is ripe.'

I stood there as still asleep. 'Announced for today?' I counted over again the time—he was right. I had constantly miscalculated a day. I sought with the right hand in my bosom for my purse—he guessed my meaning, and stepped two paces backwards.

'No, Count, that is in too good hands, keep you that.' I stared at him with eyes of inquiring wonder, and he proceeded: 'I request only a trifle, as a memento. You be so good as to set your name to this paper.'

On the parchment stood the words: 'By virtue of this my signature, I make over my soul to the holder of this, after its natural separation from the body.'

I gazed with speechless amazement alternately at the writing, and the grey unknown. Meanwhile with a new-made pen he had taken up a drop of blood which flowed from a fresh thorn-scratch on my hand, and presented it to me.

'Who are you then?' at length I asked him.

'What signifies it?' he replied. 'And is not that plain enough to be seen in me? A poor devil, a sort of learned man and doctor, who in return for precious arts receives from his friends poor thanks, and for himself has no other amusement on earth but to make his little experiments—but, however, sign. To the right there—Peter Schlemihl.'

I shook my head, and said, 'Pardon me, sir, I do not sign that.'

'Not?' replied he, in amaze. 'And why not?'

'It seems to me to a certain degree serious to stake my soul on my shadow.'

'So, so,' repeated he, 'serious!' and he laughed almost in my face. 'And if I might venture to ask what sort of a thing is that soul of yours? Have you ever seen it? And what do you think of doing with it when you are dead? Be glad that

you have found an amateur who in your lifetime is willing
to pay you for the bequest of this X, of this galvanic power,
or polarized activity, or whatever this silly thing may be,
with something actual; that is to say, with your real shadow,
through which you may arrive at the hand of your beloved,
and at the accomplishment of all your desires. Will you
rather push forth and deliver up that poor young creature to
that lowbred scoundrel Rascal? No, you must witness that
with your own eyes. Here, I lend you the Tarn-cap' (the
cap of invisibility)—he drew it from his pocket—'and we
will proceed unseen to the Forester's garden.'

I must confess that I was excessively ashamed of being
ridiculed by this man. I detested him from the bottom of
my heart, and I believe that this personal antipathy with-
held me, more than principle, or prejudice, from purchasing
my shadow, essential as it was, by the required signature.
The thought also was intolerable to me of making the
excursion which he proposed, in his company. To see this
abhorred sneak, this mocking kobold, step between me and
my beloved, two torn and bleeding hearts, revolted my
innermost feeling. I regarded what was past as predestined,
and my wretchedness as unchangeable, and turning to the
man I said to him:

'Sir, I have sold you my shadow for this, in itself, most
excellent purse, and I have sufficiently repented of it. Let
the bargain be at an end, in God's name!' He shook his

head, and made a very gloomy face. I continued: 'I will then sell you nothing further of mine, even for this offered price of my shadow; and, therefore, I shall sign nothing. From this you may understand that the cap-wearing to which you invite me, must be much more amusing for you than for me. Excuse me, therefore, and as it cannot now be otherwise, let us part.'

'It grieves me, Monsieur Schlemihl, that you obstinately decline the business which I propose to you. Perhaps another time I may be more fortunate. Till our speedy meeting again!—A propos.—Permit me yet to show you that the things which I purchase, I by no means suffer to grow mouldy, but honourably preserve, and that they are well used by me.'

With that, he drew my shadow out of his pocket, and with a dextrous throw unfolding it on the heath, spread it out on the sunny side of his feet, so that he walked between two attendant shadows, his own and mine, for mine must equally obey him, and accommodate itself to and follow all his movements.

When I once saw my poor shadow again, after so long an absence, and beheld it degraded to so vile a service, whilst I, on its account, was in such unspeakable trouble, my heart broke, and I began bitterly to weep. The detested wretch swaggered with the plunder snatched from me, and impudently renewed his proposal.

'You can yet have it. A stroke of the pen and you snatch therewith the poor and unhappy Mina from the claws of the villain into the arms of the most honoured Count—as observed, only a stroke of the pen.'

My tears burst forth with fresh impetuosity, but I turned away, and motioned to him to withdraw himself. Bendel, who filled with anxiety had traced me to this spot, at this moment arrived. When the kind, good soul found me weeping, and saw my shadow, which could not be mistaken, in the power of the mysterious grey man, he immediately resolved, was it even by force, to restore to me the possession of my property, and as he did not understand going much about with tender phrases, he immediately assaulted the man with words, and without much asking, ordered him bluntly to allow that which was my own, instantly to follow me. Instead of answer, he turned his back, and went. But Bendel up with his buckthorn cudgel which he carried, and following on his heels, without mercy, and with reiterated commands to give up the shadow, made him feel the full force of his vigorous arm. He, as accustomed to such handling, ducked his head, set up his shoulders, and with silent and deliberate steps pursued his way over the heath, at once going off with my shadow and my faithful servant. I long heard the heavy sounds roll over the waste, till they were finally lost in the distance. I was alone, as before, with my misery.

'. . . the full force of his vigorous arm.'

CHAPTER VI

LEFT alone on the wild heath, I gave free current to my countless tears, relieving my heart from an ineffably weary weight. But I saw no bound, no outlet, no end to my intolerable misery, and I drank besides with savage thirst of the fresh poison which the unknown had poured into my wounds. When I called up the image of Mina before my soul, and the dear, sweet form appeared pale and in tears, as I saw her last in my shame, then stepped the shadow of the impudent and mocking Rascal between her and me; I covered my face and fled through the wild. But the hideous apparition left me not, but pursued me in my flight, till I sank breathless on the ground, and moistened it with a fresh torrent of tears.

And all for a shadow. And this shadow a pen-stroke had obtained for me. I thought on the strange proposition and my refusal. All was chaos in me. I had no longer either judgement or mastership of thought.

The day went over. I stilled my hunger with wild fruits; my thirst in the nearest mountain stream. The night fell; I lay down beneath a tree. The damp morning awoke me out of a heavy sleep in which I heard myself rattle in the throat as in death. Bendel must have lost all trace of me, and it rejoiced me to think so. I would not return again amongst men before whom I fled in terror, like the timid game of the mountains. Thus I lived through three weary days.

On the fourth morning I found myself on a sandy plain bright with the sun and sate on the fragment of a rock in its beams, for I loved now to enjoy its long-withheld countenance. I still fed my heart with its despair. A light rustle startled me. Ready for flight I threw round me a hurried glance—I saw no one, but in the sunny sand there glided past me a human shadow, not unlike my own, which wandering there alone, seemed to have got away from its possessor. There awoke in me a mighty yearning. 'Shadow,' said I, 'dost thou seek thy master? I will be he,' and I sprang forward to seize it. I thought that if I succeeded in treading on it so that its feet touched mine, it probably would remain hanging there, and in time accommodate itself to me.

The shadow, on my moving, fled before me, and I was compelled to begin a strenuous chase of the light fugitive, for which the thought of rescuing myself from my fearful condition could have alone endowed me with the requisite vigour. It flew towards a wood, at a great distance, in which I must, of necessity, have lost it. I perceived this—a horror convulsed my heart, inflamed my desire, added wings to my speed; I gained evidently on the shadow, I came continually nearer, I must certainly reach it. Suddenly it stopped, and turned towards me. Like a lion on his prey, I shot with a mighty spring forwards to make seizure of it— and dashed unexpectedly against a hard and bodily object. Invisibly I received the most unprecedented blows on the ribs that mortal man probably ever received.

The effect of the terror in me was convulsively to close my arms, and firmly to enclose that which stood unseen before me. In the rapid transaction, I plunged forward to the ground, but backwards and under me was a man whom I had embraced and who now first became visible.

The whole occurrence became now very naturally explicable to me. The man must have carried the invisible bird's nest which renders him who holds it, but not his shadow, imperceptible, and had now cast it away. I glanced round, soon discovered the shadow of the invisible nest itself, leaped up and towards it, and did not miss the precious prize. Invisible and shadowless, I held the nest in my hand.

The man swiftly springing up, gazing round instantly after his fortunate conqueror, descried on the wide sunny plain neither him nor his shadow, for which he sought with especial avidity. For that I was myself entirely shadowless he had had no leisure to remark, nor could he imagine such a thing. Having convinced himself that every trace had vanished, he turned his hand against himself, and tore his hair. To me, however, the acquired treasure had given the power and desire to mix again amongst men. I did not want for self-satisfying palliatives for my base robbery, or rather I had no need of them, and to escape from every thought of the kind, I hastened away, not even looking round at the unhappy one, whose deploring voice I long heard resounding behind me. Thus, at least, appeared to me the circumstances at the time.

I was on fire to proceed to the Forester's garden, and there myself to discern the truth of what the Detested One had told me. I knew not, however, where I was. I climbed the next hill, in order to look round over the country, and perceived from its summit the near city, and the Forester's garden lying at my feet. My heart beat violently, and tears of another kind than what I had till now shed, rushed into my eyes. I should see her again. Anxious desire hastened my steps down the most direct path. I passed unseen some peasants who came out of the city. They were talking of me, of Rascal and the Chief Forester; I would hear nothing, I hurried past.

I entered the garden, all the tremor of expectation in my bosom. I seemed to hear laughter near me. I shuddered, threw a rapid glance round me, but could discover nobody. I advanced farther. I seemed to perceive a sound as of man's steps at hand, but there was nothing to be seen. I believed myself deceived by my ear. It was yet early, no one in Count Peter's arbour; the garden still empty. I traversed the well-known paths. I penetrated to the very front of the dwelling. The same noise more distinctly followed me. I seated myself with an agonized heart on a bench which stood in the sunny space before the house-door. It seemed as if I had heard the unseen kobold laughing in mockery seat himself near me. The key turned in the door, it opened, and the Forester issued forth with papers in his hand. A mist seemed to envelop my head. I looked up, and—horror! the man in the grey coat sate by me, gazing on me with a satanic leer. He had drawn his Tarn-cap at once over his head and mine; at his feet lay his and my shadow peaceably by each other. He played negligently with the well-known paper which he held in his hand, and as the Chief Forester busied with his documents, went to and fro in the shadow of the arbour, he stooped familiarly to my ear, and whispered in it these words:

'So then you have notwithstanding accepted my invitation, and here sit we for once two heads under one cap. All right! all right! But now give me my bird's nest again; you have no further occasion for it, and are too honourable a man to wish to withhold it from me; but there needs no thanks, I assure you that I have lent it you with the most hearty goodwill.'

He took it unceremoniously out of my hand, put it in his pocket, and laughed at me, and that so loud that the Chief Forester himself looked round at the noise. I sate there as if changed to stone.

'But you must allow,' continued he, 'that such a cap is much more convenient. It covers not only your person but your shadow at the same time, and as many others as you have a mind to take with you. See you, today again, I conduct two of them—' he laughed again. 'Mark this, Schlemihl, what we at first won't do with a good will, that will we in the end be compelled to. I still fancy you will buy that thing from me, take back the bride (for it is yet time) and we leave Rascal dangling on the gallows, an easy thing for us so long as rope is to be had. Hear you—I will give you also my cap into the bargain.'

The mother came forth, and the conversation began.

'How goes it with Mina?'

'She weeps.'

'Silly child! it cannot be altered!'

'Certainly not; but to give her to another so soon.—Oh man! Thou art cruel to thy own child.'

'No, mother; that thou quite mistakest. When she, even before she has wept out her childish tears, finds herself the wife of a very rich and honourable man, she will awake comforted out of her trouble as out of a dream, and thank God and us, that wilt thou see!'

'God grant it!'

'She possesses, now indeed, a very respectable property; but after the stir that this unlucky affair with the adventurer has made, canst thou believe that a partner so suitable as

Mr. Rascal could be readily found for her? Dost thou know what a fortune Mr. Rascal possesses? He has paid six millions for estates here in the country free from all debts. I have had the title deeds in my hands! He it was who everywhere had the start of me; and besides this, has in his possession bills on Thomas John for about five and a half millions.'

'He must have stolen enormously.'

'What talk is that again! He has wisely saved what would otherwise have been lavished away.'

'A man that has worn livery.'

'Stupid stuff! he has, however, an unblemished shadow.'

'Thou art right, but—'

The man in the grey coat laughed and looked at me. The door opened and Mina came forth. She supported herself on the arm of a chambermaid, silent tears rolled down her lovely pale cheeks. She seated herself on a stool which was placed for her under the lime trees, and her father took a chair by her. He tenderly took her hand, and addressed her with tender words, while she began violently to weep.

'Thou art my good, dear child, and thou wilt be reasonable, wilt not wish to distress thy old father, who seeks only thy happiness. I can well conceive it, dear heart, that it has sadly shaken thee. Thou art wonderfully escaped from thy misfortunes! Before we discovered the scandalous imposition, thou hadst loved this unworthy one greatly; see,

Mina, I know it, and upbraid thee not for it. I myself, dear child, also loved him so long as I looked upon him as a great gentleman. But now thou seest how different all has turned out. What! every poodle has his own shadow, and should my dear child have a husband—no! thou thinkst indeed no more about him. Listen, Mina. Now a man solicits thy hand, who does not shun the sunshine, an honourable man, who truly is no prince, but who possesses ten millions; ten times more property than thou; a man who will make my dear child happy. Answer me not, make no opposition, be my good, dutiful daughter, let thy loving father care for thee, and dry thy tears. Promise me to give thy hand to Mr. Rascal. Say, wilt thou promise me this?'

She answered with a faint voice: 'I have no will, no wish further on the earth. Happen with me what my father will.'

At this moment Mr. Rascal was announced, and stepped impudently into the circle. Mina lay in a swoon. My detested companion glanced archly at me, and whispered in hurried words:

'And that can you endure? What then flows instead of blood in your veins?' He scratched with a hasty movement a slight wound in my hand, blood flowed, and he continued: 'Actually red blood! So sign then!'

I had the parchment and the pen in my hand.

CHAPTER VII

MY WISH, dear Chamisso, is merely to submit myself to thy judgement, not to endeavour to bias it. I have long passed the severest sentence on myself, for I have nourished the tormenting worm in my heart. It hovered during this solemn moment of my life incessantly before my soul, and I could only lift my eyes to it with a despairing glance, with humility, and contrition. Dear friend, he who in levity only sets his foot out of the right road, is unawares conducted into other paths, which draw him downwards, and ever downwards; he then sees in vain the guiding stars glitter in heaven; there remains to him no choice; he must descend unpausingly the declivity, and become a voluntary sacrifice to Nemesis. After the precipitate false step which had laid the curse upon me, I had, sinning through love, forced myself into the fortunes of another being, and what remained for me but that where I sowed destruction, where speedy salvation was demanded of me, I should blindly rush forward to the rescue?—for the last hour struck! Think not so meanly of me, my Adalbert, as to imagine that I should have regarded any price that was demanded as too high, that I should have begrudged anything which was mine more even than my gold. No, Adalbert! but my soul was possessed with the most unconquerable hatred of this mysterious sneaker along crooked paths. I might do him injustice, but every degree of association with him maddened me. And here stepped forth, as so frequently in my life, and as especially often in the history of the world, an event instead of an action. Since then I have achieved reconciliation with myself. I have learned, in the first place, to reverence Necessity; and what is more than the action performed, the event accomplished; her property. Then I have learned to venerate this Necessity as a wise Providence, which lives through that great collective Machine in which we officiate simply as co-operating, impelling and impelled wheels. What shall be, must be; what should be, happened, and not without that providence, which I ultimately learned to reverence in my own fate, and in the fate of her on whom mine thus impinged.

I know not whether I shall ascribe it to the excitement of my soul under the impulse of such mighty sensations; or to the exhaustion of my physical strength, which during the last days such unwonted privations had enfeebled; or whether, finally, to the desolating commotion which the presence of this grey fiend excited in my whole nature; be that as it may, as I was on the point of signing, I fell into a deep swoon, and lay a long time as in the arms of death.

Stamping of feet and curses were the first sounds which struck my ear, as I returned to consciousness. I opened my

eyes; it was dark; my detested attendant was busied scold-
ing about me.

'Is not that to behave like an old woman? Up with you,
man! and complete off-hand what you have resolved on, if
you have not taken another thought and had rather blubber.'

I raised myself with difficulty from the ground and gazed
in silence around me. It was late in the evening; festive
music resounded from the Forester's brightly illuminated
house; various groups of people wandered through the
garden walks. One couple came near in conversation, and
seated themselves on the bench which I had just quitted.
They talked of the union this morning solemnized between
Mr. Rascal and the daughter of the house. So then it had
taken place!

I tore the Tarn-cap of the already vanished Unknown
from my head, and hastened in brooding silence towards
the garden gate, plunging myself into the deepest night of
the thicket, and striking along the path past Count Peter's
arbour. But invisibly my tormenting spirit accompanied
me, pursuing me with keenest reproaches.

'These then are one's thanks for the pains which one has
taken to support Monsieur, who has weak nerves, through
the long precious day. And one shall act the fool in the
play. Good, Mr. Wronghead, fly you from me if you please,
but we are, nevertheless, inseparable. You have my gold
and I your shadow, and this will allow us no repose. Did

anybody ever hear of a shadow forsaking its master? Yours draws me after you till you take it again into favour, and I get rid of it. What you have hesitated to do out of fresh pleasure, will you, only too late, be compelled to seek through new weariness and disgust. One cannot escape one's fate.'

He continued speaking in the same tone. I fled in vain; he relaxed not, but ever present insultingly talked of gold and shadow. I could come to no single thought of my own.

I struck through unfrequented ways towards my house. When I stood before it, and gazed at it, I could scarcely recognize it. No light shone through the dashed-in windows. The doors were closed; no throng of servants was moving therein. There was a laugh near me.

'Ha! ha! so goes it! But you'll probably find your Bendel at home, for he was the other day purposely sent back so weary that he has most likely kept his bed since.' He laughed again. 'He will have a story to tell! Well then, for the present, good night! We meet speedily again!'

I had rung repeatedly; light appeared; Bendel demanded from within who rang. When the good man recognized my voice, he could scarcely restrain his joy. The door flew open, and we stood weeping in each other's arms. I found him greatly changed, weak, and ill; but for me, my hair was become quite grey!

'*I struck through unfrequented ways.*'

He conducted me through the desolated rooms to an inner apartment which had been spared. He brought food and wine, and we seated ourselves and he again began to weep. He related to me that he the other day had cudgelled the grey-clad man whom he had encountered with my shadow, so long and so far that he had lost all trace of me, and had sunk to the earth in utter fatigue. That after this, as he could not find me, he returned home, whither presently the mob, at Rascal's instigation, came rushing in fury, dashed in the windows, and gave full play to their lust of demolition. Thus did they to their benefactor. The servants had fled various ways. The police had ordered me, as a suspicious person, to quit the city, and had allowed only four and twenty hours in which to evacuate their juris-diction. To that which I already knew of Rascal's affluence and marriage, he had yet much to add. This scoundrel, from whom all had proceeded that had been done against me, must, from the beginning, have been in possession of my secret. It appeared that, attracted by gold, he had con-trived to thrust himself upon me, and at the very first had procured a key to the gold-cupboard, where he had laid the foundation of that fortune, whose augmentation he could now afford to despise.

All this Bendel narrated to me with abundant tears, and then wept for joy that he again beheld me, again had me; and that after he had long doubted whither this misfortune might have led me, he saw me bear it so calmly and collectedly; for such an aspect had despair now assumed in me. I beheld my misery of giant size unchangeably before me; I had wept out to it my last tear; not another cry could be extorted from my heart; I presented to it my bare head with chill indifference.

'Bendel,' I said, 'thou knowest my lot. Not without earlier blame has my heavy punishment befallen me. Thou, innocent man, shalt no longer bind thy destiny to mine. I do not desire it. I ride tonight still forward: saddle me a horse; I ride alone; thou remainest: it is my will. Here still must remain some chests of gold; that retain thou; but I will alone wander incessantly through the world: but if ever a happier hour should smile upon me, and fortune look on me with reconciled eyes, then will I remember thee, for I have wept upon thy firmly faithful bosom in heavy and agonizing hours.'

With a broken heart was this honest man compelled to obey this last command of his master, at which his soul shrunk in terror. I was deaf to his prayers, to his representations, blind to his tears; he brought me out my steed. Once more I pressed the weeping man to my bosom; sprung into the saddle, and under the shroud of night hastened from the grave of my existence, regardless which way my horse conducted me, since I had longer on the earth no aim, no wish, no hope.

CHAPTER VIII

A PEDESTRIAN soon joined me who begged, after he had walked for some time by the side of my horse, that as we went the same way, he might be allowed to lay a cloak which he carried on the steed behind me. I permitted it in silence. He thanked me with easy politeness for the trifling service; praised my horse, and thence took occasion to extol the happiness and power of the rich, and let himself, I know not how, fall into a kind of monologue, in which he had me now merely for a listener.

He unfolded his views of life and of the world, and came very soon upon metaphysics, in which the ultimate pretension extended to the discovery of the word that should solve all mysteries. He stated his premises with great clearness, and proceeded to the proofs.

Thou knowest, my friend, that I have clearly discovered, since I have run through the schools of the philosophers, that I have by no means a turn for philosophical speculations, and that I have totally renounced for myself this field. Since then I have left many things to themselves; abandoned the desire to know and to comprehend many things; and as thou thyself advised me, have, trusting to my common sense, followed as far as I was able the voice within me on the direct course. Now this rhetorician seemed to me to raise with great talent a firmly put-together fabric, which was at once self-based and self-supported, and stood as by an innate necessity. I missed, however, in it completely, what most of all I was desirous to find, and so it became for me merely a work of art, whose ornamental compactness and completeness served only to charm the eye; nevertheless I listened willingly to the eloquent man who drew my attention from my griefs to himself; and I would have gladly yielded myself wholly up to him, had he captivated my heart as much as my understanding.

Meanwhile the time had passed, and unobserved the dawn had already enlightened the heaven. I was horrified as I looked suddenly up, and saw the pomp of colours unfold itself in the east, which announced the approach of the sun, while at this hour in which the shadows ostentatiously display themselves in their greatest extent, there was no protection from it; no refuge in the open country to be descried. And I was not alone! I cast a glance at my companion, and was again terror-struck. It was no other than the man in the grey coat!

He smiled at my alarm, and went on without allowing me to get in a word. 'Let, however, as is the way of the world, our mutual advantage for a while unite us. It is all in good time for separating. The road here along the mountain-range, though you have not yet thought of it, is, nevertheless, the only one into which you could prudently have struck. Down into the valley you may not venture; and still less will you desire to return again over the heights, whence you are come; and this is also exactly my way. I see that you already turn pale before the rising sun. I will, for the time we keep company, lend you your shadow, and you, on that account, tolerate me in your society. You have no longer your Bendel with you, I will do you good service. You do not like me, and I am sorry for it; but, notwithstanding, you can make use of me. The devil is not so black as he is painted. Yesterday you vexed me, it is true, I will not upbraid you with it today; and I have already shortened the way hither for you; that you must allow. Only just take your shadow again awhile on trial.'

The sun had ascended; people appeared on the road; I accepted, though with internal repugnance, the proposal. Smiling he let my shadow glide to the ground, which immediately took its place on that of the horse, and trotted gaily by my side. I was in the strangest state of mind. I rode past a group of country-people, who made way for a man of consequence, reverently, and with bared heads. I rode on, and gazed with greedy eyes and a palpitating heart on this my quondam shadow which I had now borrowed from a stranger, yes, from an enemy.

The man went carelessly near me, and even whistled a tune. He on foot, I on horseback; a dizziness seized me;

the temptation was too great; I suddenly turned the reins; clapped spurs to the horse, and struck, at full speed, into a side-path. But I carried not off the shadow, which at the turning glided from the horse, and awaited its lawful possessor on the highroad. I was compelled with shame to turn back. The man in the grey coat when he had calmly finished his tune, laughed at me, set the shadow right again for me; and informed me that it would then only hang fast and remain with me when I was disposed to become the rightful proprietor.

'I hold you,' continued he, 'fast by the shadow, and you cannot escape me. A rich man like you needs a shadow, it cannot be otherwise, and you only are to blame that you did not perceive that sooner.'

I continued my journey on the same road; the comforts and the splendour of life again surrounded me; I could move about free and conveniently, since I possessed a shadow, although only a borrowed one; and I everywhere inspired the respect which riches command. But I carried death in my heart. My strange companion, who gave himself out as the unworthy servant of the richest man in the world, possessed an extraordinary professional readiness, prompt and clever beyond comparison, the very model of a valet for a rich man, but he stirred not from my side, perpetually directing the conversation towards me; and continually blabbing out the most confidential matters; so that, at length, were it only to be rid of him, I resolved to settle the affair of the shadow. He was become as burthensome to me as he was hateful. I was even in fear of him. He had made me dependent on him. He held me, after he had conducted me back into the glory of the world which I had fled from. I was obliged to tolerate his eloquence upon myself, and felt, in fact, that he was in the right. A rich man in the world must have a shadow, and so soon as I desired to command the rank which he had contrived again to make necessary to me, I saw but one issue. By this, however, I stood fast—after having sacrificed my love, after my life had been blighted, I would never sign away my soul to this creature, for all the shadows in the world. I knew not how it would end.

We sate, one day, before a cave which the strangers who frequent these mountains are accustomed to visit. We heard there the rush of subterranean streams roaring up from immeasurable depths, and the stone cast in seemed, in its resounding fall, to find no bottom. He painted to me, as he often did, with a vivid power of imagination and in the lustrous charms of the most brilliant colours, the most carefully finished pictures of what I might achieve in the world by virtue of my purse, if I had but once my shadow in my possession. With my elbows rested on my knees, I kept my face concealed in my hands, and listened to the false one, my heart divided between the seduction and my own strong will. In such an inward conflict I could no longer contain myself, and the deciding strife began.

'You appear, sir, to forget that I have indeed allowed you, upon certain conditions, to remain in my company, but that I have reserved my perfect freedom.'

'If you command it I pack up.'

He was accustomed to menace. I was silent; he began immediately to roll up my shadow. I turned pale, but I let it proceed. There followed a long pause; he first broke it.

'You cannot bear me, sir. You hate me; I know it; yet why do you hate me? Is it because you attacked me on the highway, and sought to deprive me by violence of my bird's nest? Or is it because you have endeavoured, in a thievish manner, to cheat me out of my property, the shadow, which was entrusted to you entirely on your honour? I, for my part, do not, therefore, hate you. I find it quite natural that you should seek to avail yourself of all your advantages, cunning, and power. For the rest, that you have the very strictest principles; and that you think like honour itself, is a taste that you have—against which I have nothing to say. In fact, I think not so strictly as you; I merely act as you think. Or have I at any time pressed my finger on your throat in order to bring to me your most precious soul, for which I have a fancy? Have I, on account of my bartered purse, let a servant loose on you? Have I sought thus to swindle you out of it?'

I had nothing to oppose to this, and he proceeded.

'Very good, sir! very good! you cannot endure me; I know that very well, and am by no means angry with you for it. We must part, that is clear, and, in fact, you begin to be very wearisome to me. In order then, to rid you of my further, shame-inspiring presence, I counsel you once more purchase this thing from me.'

I extended to him the purse. 'At that price?'

'No!'

I sighed deeply, and added, 'Be it so then. I insist, sir, that we part, and that you no longer obstruct my path in a world which, it is to be hoped, has room enough in it for us both.'

He smiled, and replied, 'I go, sir; but first let me instruct you how you may ring for me when you desire to see again your most devoted servant. You have only to shake your purse, so that the eternal gold-pieces therein jingle, and the sound will instantly attract me. Everyone thinks of his own advantage in this world. You see that I at the same time am thoughtful of yours, since I reveal to you a new power. Oh! this purse!—had the moths already devoured your shadow, that would still constitute a strong bond between us. Enough, you have me in my gold. Should you have any commands, even when far off, for your servant, you know that I can show myself very active in the service of my friends, and the rich stand particularly well with me. You have seen it yourself. Only your shadow, sir—allow me to tell you that—never again, except on one sole condition.'

Forms of the past time swept before my soul. I demanded hastily: 'Had you a signature from Mr. John?'

He smiled. 'With so good a friend it was by no means necessary.'

'Where is he? By God I will know it!'

He plunged hesitatingly his hand into his pocket, and, dragged thence by the hair, appeared Thomas John's ghastly, disfigured form, and the blue death-lips moved themselves with heavy words—'*Justo judicio Dei judicatus sum; justo judicio Dei condemnatus sum.*'

I shuddered with horror, and dashing the ringing purse into the abyss, I spoke to him the last words:

'I adjure thee, horrible one, in the name of God! take thyself hence, and never again show thyself in my sight!'

He arose gloomily, and instantly vanished behind the masses of rock which bounded this wild, overgrown spot.

'*Lovely shapes blended themselves before me in charming dance.*'

CHAPTER IX

I SATE there without shadow and without money, but a heavy weight was taken from my bosom. I was calm. Had I not lost my love, or had I in that loss felt myself free from blame, I believe that I should have been happy; but I knew not, however, what I should do. I examined my pockets; I found yet several gold pieces there; I counted them and laughed. I had my horses below at the inn; I was ashamed of returning thither; I must, at least, wait till the sun was gone down; it stood yet high in the heaven. I laid myself down in the shade of the nearest trees, and fell calmly asleep.

Lovely shapes blended themselves before me in charming dance into a pleasing dream. Mina with a flower-wreath in her hair floated by me, and smiled kindly upon me. The noble Bendel also was crowned with flowers, and went past with a friendly greeting. I saw many besides, and I believe thee too, Chamisso, in the distant throng. A bright light appeared, but no one had a shadow, and what was stranger, it had by no means a bad effect. Flowers and songs, love and joy under groves of palm. I could neither hold fast nor single out the moving, lightly floating, loveable forms; but I knew that I dreamed such a dream with joy, and was careful to avoid waking. I was already awake, but still kept my eyes closed in order to retain the fading apparitions longer before my soul.

I finally opened my eyes; the sun stood still high in the heaven, but in the east; I had slept through the night. I took it for a sign that I should not return to the inn. I gave up readily as lost, what I yet possessed there, and determined to strike on foot into a neighbouring path, which led along the wood-grown feet of the mountains, leaving it secretly to fate to fulfil what it had yet in store for me. I looked not behind me, and thought not even of applying to Bendel, whom I left rich behind me, and which I could readily have done. I considered the new character which I should support in the world. My dress was very modest. I had on an old black Polonaise, which I had already worn in Berlin, and which, I know not how, had first come again into my hands for this journey. I had also a travelling-cap on my head, a pair of old boots on my feet. I arose, and cut me on the spot a knotty stick as a memorial, and advanced at once on my wandering.

I met in the wood an old peasant who friendlily greeted me, and with whom I entered into conversation. I inquired, like an inquisitive traveller, first the way, then about the country and its inhabitants, the productions of the mountains, and many such things. He answered my questions sensibly and loquaciously. We came to the bed of a mountain torrent, which had spread its devastations over a wide tract of the forest. I shuddered involuntarily at the sun-bright space, and allowed the countryman to go first; but in the midst of this dangerous spot, he stood still, and turned to relate to me the history of this desolation. He saw immediately my defect, and paused in the midst of his discourse.

'But how does that happen—the gentleman has actually no shadow!'

'Alas! alas!' replied I sighing, 'during a long and severe illness, my hair, nails, and shadow fell off. See, father, at my age, my hair, which is renewed again, is quite white, the nails very short, and the shadow—that will never grow again.'

'Ay! ay!' responded the old man, shaking his head, 'no shadow, that is bad! That was a bad illness that the gentle-man had.'

But he continued not his narrative, and at the next cross way which presented itself, he left me without saying a word. Bitter tears trembled anew upon my cheeks, and my cheerfulness was gone.

I pursued my way with a sorrowful heart, and sought no further the society of men. I kept myself in the darkest wood, and was many a time compelled, in order to pass over a space where the sun shone, to wait for whole hours, least some human eye should forbid me the transit. In the evening

I sought for a small inn in the villages. I went particularly in quest of a mine in the mountains where I hoped to get work under the earth; since, besides that my present situation made it imperative that I should provide for my support, I had discovered that the most active labour alone could protect me from my own annihilating thoughts.

A few rainy days advanced me well on the way, but at the expense of my boots whose soles had been calculated for Count Peter, and not for the pedestrian labourer. I was already barefoot, I must procure a pair of new boots. The next morning I transacted this business with much gravity in a village where was held a Wake, and where in a booth old and new boots stood for sale. I selected and bargained long. I was forced to deny myself a new pair, which I would gladly have had, but the extravagant demand frightened me. I therefore contented myself with an old pair, which were yet good and strong, and which the handsome, blond-haired boy who kept the stall, for present cash payment, handed to me with a friendly smile, and wished me good luck on my journey. I put them on at once, and left the place by the northern gate.

I was sunk very deep in my thoughts, and scarcely saw where I set my feet, for I was pondering on the mine which I hoped to reach by evening, and where I hardly knew how I should propose myself. I had not advanced two hundred strides when I observed that I had got out of the way.

I therefore looked round me, and found myself in a wild and ancient forest, where the axe appeared never to have been wielded. I pressed forward still a few steps, and beheld myself in the midst of desert rocks which were overgrown only with moss and lichens, and between which lay fields of snow and ice. The air was intensely cold; I looked round —the wood had vanished behind me. I took a few strides more—and around me reigned the silence of death: boundlessly extended itself the ice whereon I stood, and on which rested a thick, heavy fog. The sun stood blood-red on the edge of the horizon. The cold was insupportable. I knew not what had happened to me; the benumbing frost compelled me to hasten my steps; I heard alone the roar of distant waters; a step, and I was on the ice-margin of an ocean. Innumerable herds of seals plunged rushing before me in the flood. I pursued this shore; I saw again naked rocks, land, birch and pine forests; I now advanced for a few minutes right onwards. It was stifling hot. I looked round—I stood amongst beautifully cultivated rice-fields, and beneath mulberry-trees. I seated myself in their shade; I looked at my watch; I had left the market town only a quarter of an hour before. I fancied that I dreamed; I bit my tongue to awake myself, but I was really awake. I closed my eyes in order to collect my thoughts. I heard before me singular accents pronounced through the nose. I looked up. Two Chinese, unmistakeable from their Asiatic form of countenance, if indeed I would have given no credit to their costume, addressed me in their speech with the accustomed salutations of their country. I arose and stepped two paces backward; I saw them no more. The landscape was totally changed, trees and forests instead of rice-fields. I contemplated these trees, and the plants which bloomed around me, which I recognized as the growth of south-eastern Asia. I wished to approach one of these trees—one step, and again all was changed. I marched now like a recruit who is drilled, and strode slowly, and with measured steps. Wonderfully diversified lands, rivers, meadows, mountain-chains, steppes, deserts of sand unrolled themselves before my astonished eyes. There was no doubt of it—I had seven-leagued boots on my feet.

CHAPTER X

I FELL in speechless adoration on my knees and shed tears of thankfulness, for suddenly stood my fortune clear before my soul. For early offence thrust out from the society of men, I was cast, for compensation, upon Nature, which I ever loved; the earth was given me as a rich garden, study for the object and strength of my life, and science for its goal. It was no resolution which I adopted. I have since then, with severe, unremitted diligence, striven faithfully to represent what then stood clear and perfect before my eye, and my satisfaction has depended on the agreement of the demonstration with the original.

I prepared without hesitation, with a hasty survey, to take possession of the field which I should hereafter reap. I stood on the heights of Tibet, and the sun, which had risen upon me only a few hours before, now already stooped to the evening sky. I wandered over Asia from east to west, overtaking him in his course, and entered Africa. I gazed about me with eager curiosity, as I repeatedly traversed it in all directions. As I surveyed the ancient pyramids and temples in passing through Egypt, I descried in the desert not far from hundred-gated Thebes, the caves where the

Christian anchorites once dwelt. It was suddenly firm and clear in me—here is thy home! I selected one of the most concealed which was at the same time spacious, convenient and inaccessible to the jackalls, for my future abode and again went forward.

I passed at the pillars of Hercules, over to Europe, and, when I had reviewed the southern and northern provinces, I crossed from northern Asia over the polar glaciers to Greenland and America; traversed both parts of that continent, and the winter which already reigned in the south drove me speedily back northwards from Cape Horn.

I tarried awhile till it was day in eastern Asia, and after some repose, continued my wandering. I traced through both Americas the mountain chain which comprehends the highest known inequalities on our globe. I stalked slowly and cautiously from summit to summit, now over flaming volcanoes, now snow-crowned peaks, often breathing with difficulty; when reaching Mount Elias, I sprang across Behring's Straits to Asia. I followed the western shores, in their manifold windings, and examined with especial care which of the islands there located were accessible to me. From the peninsula of Malacca my boots carried me to Sumatra, Java, Bali and Lamboc. I attempted often with danger, and always in vain, a north-west passage over the lesser islets and rocks with which this sea is studded to Borneo and the other islands of this Archipelago. I was compelled to abandon the hope. At length I seated myself on the extremest part of Lamboc, and gazing towards the south and the east, wept, as at the fast closed grating of my prison, that I had so soon discovered my limits. New Holland so extraordinary, and so essentially necessary to the comprehension of the earth and its sun-woven garment, of the vegetable and the animal world, with the South Sea and its zoophyte islands, was interdicted to me, and thus, at the very outset, all that I should gather and build up was destined to remain a mere fragment! Oh, my Adalbert, what, after all, are the endeavours of men!

Often did I in the severest winter of the southern hemisphere, endeavour, passing the polar glaciers westward, to leave behind me those two hundred strides out from Cape Horn which sundered me probably from Van Diemen's Land, and New Holland, regardless of my return, or whether this dismal region should close upon me as my coffin lid, making desperate leaps from ice-drift to ice-drift and bidding defiance to the cold and the sea. In vain; I never reached New Holland, but every time I came back to Lamboc, seated myself on its extremest peak, and wept again, with my face turned towards the south and east, as at the fast closed bars of my prison.

I tore myself at length from this spot, and returned with a sorrowful heart into inner Asia. I traversed that farther, pursuing the morning dawn westward, and came yet in the night to my proposed home in the Thebais, which I had touched upon in the afternoon of the day before.

As soon as I was somewhat rested, and when it was day again in Europe, I made it my first care to procure everything which I wanted. First of all, stop-shoes; for I had experienced how inconvenient it was when I wished to examine near objects, not to be able to slacken my stride, except by pulling off my boots. A pair of slippers drawn over them had completely the effect which I anticipated, and later I always carried two pairs, since I sometimes threw them from my feet, without having time to pick them up again, when lions, men, or hyaenas startled me from my botanizing. My very excellent watch was, for the short duration of my passage, a capital chronometer. Besides this I needed a sextant, some scientific instruments and books.

To procure all this, I made several anxious journeys to London and Paris, which, auspiciously for me, a mist just then overshadowed. As the remains of my enchanted gold was now exhausted, I easily accomplished the payment by gathering African ivory, in which, however, I was obliged to select only the smallest tusks, as not too heavy for me. I was soon furnished and equipped with all these, and commenced immediately, as private philosopher, my new course of life.

I roamed about the earth, now determining the altitudes of mountains; now the temperature of its springs and the air; now contemplating the animal, now inquiring into the vegetable tribes. I hastened from the equator to the pole; from one world to the other, comparing facts with facts. The eggs of the African ostrich or the northern sea-fowl, and fruits, especially of the tropical palms and bananas, were even my ordinary food. In lieu of happiness I had tobacco, and of human society and the ties of love, one faithful poodle, which guarded my cave in the Thebais, and when I returned home with fresh treasures, sprang joyfully towards me, and gave me still a human feeling, that I was not alone on the earth. An adventure was yet destined to conduct me back amongst mankind.

CHAPTER XI

A S I ONCE scotched my boots on the shores of the north, and gathered lichens and sea-weed, an ice-bear came unawares upon me round the corner of a rock. Flinging off my slippers, I would step over to an opposite island, to which a naked crag which protruded midway from the waves offered me a passage. I stepped with one foot firmly on the rock, and plunged over on the other side into the sea, one of my slippers having unobserved remained fast on the foot.

The excessive cold seized on me; I with difficulty rescued my life from this danger; and the moment I reached land, I ran with the utmost speed to the Lybian deserts in order to dry myself in the sun, but as I was here exposed, it burned me so furiously on the head that I staggered back again very ill towards the north. I sought to relieve myself by rapid motion, and ran with swift, uncertain steps from west to east, from east to west. I found myself now in the day, now in the night; now in summer and now in the winter's cold.

I know not how long I thus reeled about on the earth. A burning fever glowed in my veins; with deepest distress I felt my senses forsaking me. As mischief would have it, in

'A burning fever glowed in my veins; with deepest distress I felt my senses forsaking me.'

my incautious career, I now trod on someone's foot; I must have hurt him; I received a heavy blow, and fell to the ground.

When I again returned to consciousness, I lay comfortably in a good bed, which stood amongst many other beds in a handsome hall. Some one sate at my head; people went through the hall from one bed to another. They came to mine, and spake together about me. They stiled me *Number Twelve*; and on the wall at my feet stood, yes certainly it was no delusion, I could distinctly read on a black tablet of marble in great golden letters, quite correctly written, my name:

PETER SCHLEMIHL

On the tablet beneath my name were two other rows of letters, but I was too weak to put them together. I again closed my eyes.

I heard something of which the subject was Peter Schlemihl read aloud, and articulately, but I could not collect the sense. I saw a friendly man, and a very lovely woman in black dress appear at my bedside. The forms were not strange to me, and yet I could not recognize them.

Some time went over, and I recovered my strength. I was called *Number Twelve*, and *Number Twelve*, on account of his long beard, passed for a Jew, on which account, however, he was not at all the less carefully treated. That he had no shadow appeared to have been unobserved. My boots, as I was assured, were, with all that I had brought hither, in good keeping, in order to be restored to me on my recovery. The place in which I lay ill was called the SCHLEMIH-LIUM. What was daily read aloud concerning Peter Schlemihl, was an exhortation to pray for him as the Founder and Benefactor of this institution. The friendly man whom I had seen by my bed was Bendel; the lovely woman was Mina.

I recovered unrecognized in the Schlemihlium; and learned yet further that I was in Bendel's native city, where, with the remains of my otherwise unblessed gold, he had in my name founded this hospital where the unhappy blessed me, and himself maintained its superintendence. Mina was a widow. An unfortunate criminal process had cost Mr. Rascal his life, and her the greater part of her property. Her parents were no more. She lived here as a pious widow, and practised works of mercy.

Once she conversed with Mr. Bendel at the bedside of *Number Twelve.*

'Why, noble lady, will you so often expose yourself to the bad atmosphere which prevails here? Does fate then deal so hardly with you that you wish to die?'

'No, Mr. Bendel, since I have dreamed out my long dream, and have awoke in myself, all is well with me; since then I crave not, and fear not death. Since then, I reflect calmly on the past and the future. Is it not also with a still and inward happiness that you now, in so devout a manner, serve your master and friend?'

'Thank God, yes, noble lady. But we have seen wonderful things; we have unwarily drunk much good, and bitter woe out of the full cup. Now it is empty, and we may believe that the whole has been only a trial; and armed with wise discernment, await the real beginning. The real beginning is of another fashion; and we wish not back the first jugglery, and are on the whole glad, such as it was, to have lived through it. I feel also in me a confidence that it must now be better than formerly with our old friend.'

'In me too,' replied the lovely widow, and then passed on.

The conversation left a deep impression upon me, but I was undecided in myself, whether I should make myself known, or depart hence unrecognized. I took my resolve. I requested paper and pencil, and wrote these words:

'It is indeed better with your old friend now than formerly, and if he does penance it is the penance of reconciliation.'

Hereupon I desired to dress myself, as I found myself stronger. The key of the small wardrobe which stood near my bed was brought, and I found therein all that belonged to me. I put on my clothes, suspended my botanical case, in which I rejoiced still to find my northern lichens, round my black Polonaise, drew on my boots, laid the written paper on my bed, and, as the door opened, I was already far on the way to the Thebais.

As I took the way along the Syrian coast, on which I for the last time had wandered from home, I perceived my poor Figaro coming towards me. This excellent poodle, who had long expected his master at home, seemed to desire to trace him out. I stood still and called to him. He sprang barking towards me, with a thousand moving assurances of his inmost and most extravagant joy. I took him up under my arm, for in truth he could not follow me, and brought him with me home again.

I found all in its old order; and returned gradually, as my strength was recruited, to my former employment and mode of life, except that I kept myself for a whole year out of the, to me, wholly insupportable polar cold. And thus, my dear Chamisso, I live to this day. My boots are no worse for the wear, as that very learned work of the celebrated Tieckius, *de rebus gestis Pollicelli*, at first led me to fear. Their force remains unimpaired, my strength only decays; yet I have the comfort to have exerted it in a continuous and not fruitless pursuit of one object. I have, so far as my boots could carry me, become more fundamentally acquainted than any man before me with the earth, its shape, its elevations, its temperatures, the changes of its atmosphere, the exhibitions of its magnetic power, and the life upon it, especially in the vegetable world. The facts I have recorded with the greatest possible exactness, and in perspicuous order in several works, and stated my deductions and views briefly in several treatises. I have settled the geography of the interior of Africa, and of the northern polar regions; of the interior of Asia, and its eastern shores. My *Historia Stirpium Plantarum Utriusque Orbis* stands as a grand fragment of the *Flora Universalis Terrae,* and as a branch of my *Systema Naturae.* I believe that I have therein not merely augmented, at a moderate calculation, the amount of known species, more than one third, but have done something for the Natural System, and for the Geography of plants. I shall labour diligently at my Fauna. I shall take care that, before my death, my works shall be deposited in the Berlin University.

And thee, my dear Chamisso, have I selected as the preserver of my singular history, which, perhaps when I have vanished from the earth, may afford valuable instruction to many of its inhabitants. But thou, my friend, if thou wilt live among men, learn before all things to reverence the shadow, and then gold. Wishest thou to live only for thyself and for thy better self—oh, then!—thou needest no counsel.

EXPLICIT

The Story Classics edition of *The Wonderful History of Peter Schlemihl* is set in Ehrhardt, a Monotype face based on the type first cut in Leipzig probably towards the end of the seventeenth century although the first specimen sheet was not issued by the Ehrhardt Foundry until about 1720. The size used is twelve point with four points of leading between lines

———————

This edition has been limited to three thousand copies. Two thousand copies (numbered 1 to 2,000) are reserved for members of Story Classics and one thousand (numbered A 1 to A 1,000) are available for distribution in Great Britain

THIS IS COPY 1,026